School of Mischief

To Reuben—a boisterous and
bouncy spotty boy.

GROSSET & DUNLAP
Published by the Penguin Group
Penguin Group (USA) Inc., 375 Hudson Street, New York,
New York 10014, USA
Penguin Group (Canada), 90 Eglinton Avenue East, Suite 700,
Toronto, Ontario M4P 2Y3, Canada
(a division of Pearson Penguin Canada Inc.)
Penguin Books Ltd., 80 Strand, London WC2R 0RL, England
Penguin Group Ireland, 25 St. Stephen's Green, Dublin 2, Ireland
(a division of Penguin Books Ltd.)
Penguin Group (Australia), 250 Camberwell Road,
Camberwell, Victoria 3124, Australia
(a division of Pearson Australia Group Pty. Ltd.)
Penguin Books India Pvt. Ltd., 11 Community Centre, Panchsheel Park,
New Delhi—110 017, India
Penguin Group (NZ), 67 Apollo Drive, Rosedale, North Shore 0632, New Zealand
(a division of Pearson New Zealand Ltd.)
Penguin Books (South Africa) (Pty.) Ltd., 24 Sturdee Avenue,
Rosebank, Johannesburg 2196, South Africa

Penguin Books Ltd., Registered Offices:
80 Strand, London WC2R 0RL, England

Text copyright © 2008 Sue Bentley. Illustrations copyright © 2008 Angela Swan.
Cover illustration copyright © 2008 Andrew Farley. First printed in Great Britain in
2008 by Penguin Books Ltd. First published in the United States in 2010 by Grosset
& Dunlap, a division of Penguin Young Readers Group, 345 Hudson Street, New
York, New York 10014. GROSSET & DUNLAP is a trademark of Penguin Group
(USA) Inc. Printed in the U.S.A.

Library of Congress Cataloging-in-Publication Data is available.

ISBN 978-0-448-45067-4   10

Sue Bentley

Magic Puppy

School of Mischief

Illustrated by *Angela Swan*

Grosset & Dunlap
An Imprint of Penguin Group (USA) Inc.

Prologue

Storm padded silently across the frozen lake. The young, silver-gray wolf took a deep breath of cold air. It felt good to be back.

Suddenly, a terrifying howl rang out, echoing in the violet night sky.

"Shadow!" gasped Storm. The powerful lone wolf who had attacked the Moon-claw pack was very close. Storm should have known that it wasn't safe to return.

There was a bright flash of light and a dazzling burst of golden sparks. Where the young wolf had been standing there was now a tiny puppy with fluffy,

1

gray and white fur, a round face, and midnight blue eyes.

Storm hoped this disguise would protect him until he found a place to hide.

Over by the shore, thick clumps of bushes stuck up through the ice. Storm sped toward them, his little furry sides heaving. When he reached the bushes, Storm flattened his belly against the ice and crawled into them.

There was a crackling of broken stems nearby. A dark mass appeared and a large paw, almost as big as Storm was now, reached out and scooped him up.

Storm whimpered with terror. His claws scrabbled desperately as he was drawn backward.

"Be calm, my son," growled a deep, gentle voice. "You are safe for the moment."

"Mother!" Storm yipped with relief. His whole body wriggled and his gray and white tail twirled as he licked Canista's muzzle.

Canista's gold eyes softened as she smiled down at her tiny disguised cub. "I am glad to see you again, but you cannot stay. Shadow is looking for you. He wants to lead the Moon-claw pack."

Storm's lip curled, exposing needle-sharp puppy teeth. "Is it not enough that he killed my father and litter brothers and wounded you? We must fight Shadow and make him leave our lands!"

Canista shook her large head. "He is

too strong for you and I am still weak from his poisoned bite and cannot help you," she rumbled gently. "The others will not follow Shadow while you live. Go back to the other world. Return when you are wiser and stronger . . ." She bit back a wince of pain.

Storm hated to leave her, but he knew his mother was right. Opening his mouth, he huffed out a glittering puppy breath. The sparkly, golden mist whirled around Canista's injured paw and then sank into her gray fur.

"Thank you, Storm. I feel a little stronger," she breathed.

Another fierce howl rang out and there came the sound of mighty paws thundering across the ice.

"Go now! Save yourself, Storm!" urged Canista.

Storm whimpered as he felt the power building inside him. Bright gold sparks ignited in his fluffy, gray and white fur. A bright light glowed around him. And grew brighter . . .

Chapter
ONE

Julie Harding sat on the rug in her grandmother's cute apartment. Sunlight poured on to the Victorian dollhouse that stood open in front of her.

Usually, Julie loved playing with all the miniature dolls and furniture, but even that couldn't cheer her up today. She sighed as she tucked a strand of brown hair behind one ear.

"Are you all right, sweetie?" asked Granny Harding, looking up from her newspaper where she was doing sudoku puzzles.

"I was just wondering if my old
friends were missing me yet," Julie said
wistfully. It was right at the beginning of
the school summer vacation and she and
her parents had moved to be closer to
Granny Harding.

Gran put down the newspaper and
took off her glasses. "A great girl like
you! Of course they are," she said,

7

smiling. "I would expect they'll keep in touch. But you're bound to make lots of new friends when you start your new school."

"That won't be for a while," Julie grumbled.

"Time passes more quickly when you're having fun," said Gran. "Do you want to do some cooking? We could pretend we're a couple of TV chefs!"

"I don't really feel like it. Couldn't I go back to the new house? I'll play computer games or e-mail my old friends until Mom gets back."

Gran shook her head. "I'm afraid not, sweetie. We agreed that you'd stay here with me while your parents are at work."

Julie's shoulders slumped. "I am nine years old. I know tons of kids my age who take care of themselves for the whole day."

"Well, you're not going to be one of them," Gran said firmly. "If you're feeling restless you can take a walk to the store." She stood up and reached for her handbag. "Here's some money. Will you

get a loaf of bread and some milk, please?
And buy yourself a comic."

"Gra-an! No one says 'comic' anymore!"
Julie teased.

Gran's eyes sparkled. "Get a magazine,
then. Same difference, you silly girl! But if
you're not that interested . . ."

"No, I'll go," Julie said hurriedly. It
was something to do and the town store
was interesting in a weird kind of way.
It sold boring stuff like knitting wool and
dusty little cards of pins, but it also had
yummy, old-fashioned candies in big glass
jars.

Julie opened the front door. "I'll bring
you a treat back. Lemon sherbets or pear
drops?" she called over her shoulder.

"Surprise me!" Gran called.

Julie went downstairs and out of the converted shoe factory building. The store was just down the street. As she opened the door, a bell clanged loudly. A man popped his head out of a back room. "I'll just be a minute. Give me a shout when you've found what you're looking for," he called.

"Okay, fine," Julie replied, but he'd disappeared again.

Julie looked around at the cluttered shelves of the quiet, little store. There didn't seem to be anyone to talk to or to make friends with in this new town. Julie sighed as she realized she was just going to have to make do with Gran's company for the summer until her new school began.

She was wandering over to the big glass jars of candies to choose something her gran might like, when she was stopped in her path by a bright, golden flash that lit up the whole store.

Julie rubbed her eyes, blinded for a minute. One of the store's display lights must have been faulty.

When she could finally see again, Julie opened her eyes to see a realistic-looking toy sheepdog puppy. It was sitting on the shelf right in front of her, squeezed in among the glass jars. The toy was very lifelike, with fluffy, gray and white fur and sparkling midnight blue eyes peeping out from beneath a fuzzy little fringe.

"Oh, aren't you gorgeous! I wonder how much you are?" she said.

"I am not for sale!" the puppy woofed. "Can you help me, please?"

Chapter
TWO

"Wow!" Julie blinked in fascination. The cute toy puppy must have some sort of noise-activated computer chip inside. "Say something else!"

Julie leaned toward it. "Grr-uf! Grr-uf!" she said, hoping that the sound of her voice would make it speak again.

The puppy blinked and stood up, balancing carefully on the shelf. Its little tail drooped and just the end of it started wagging. "I am afraid that I do not understand you. I am Storm of the Moon-

claw pack. What is your name?"

Julie's jaw dropped and she did a double take. "You . . . you're . . . real!"

Storm nodded. "Yes, I am." He put his little head to one side and looked at her with big, serious, midnight blue eyes.

Julie swallowed, not quite sure that this was really happening. She looked up at the counter to see if the shopkeeper was watching, but he still hadn't returned from the storeroom.

Julie realized that the little puppy seemed to be waiting for her to reply. "I . . . I'm Julie. Julie Harding," she found herself gulping.

Storm dipped his fluffy little head. "I am honored to meet you, Julie," he yapped politely.

Julie was still puzzled. "Um . . . thanks. But how come you can talk? And where did you come from?"

"All of my kind can talk. I have come from another world, which is far away. I need to hide from the fierce lone wolf who attacked us—his name is Shadow," the tiny puppy told her. His furry little brow wrinkled in a frown. "Shadow wants to lead the Moon-claw pack. I am the only cub left. The other wolves are waiting for me to grow strong and become their leader."

Julie frowned, confused. "Wolves? Cub? But you're just a tiny pup–"

Storm lifted his chin. "Stand back, please. I will show you!"

There was another dazzling burst of golden light and a fountain of bright sparks sprayed out and sizzled as they trickled down all around Julie.

The tiny, cute puppy had disappeared from the shelf. Standing in the aisle before her was an impressive young silver-gray wolf with glowing midnight blue eyes and a thick neck-ruff that seemed to glitter with a thousand tiny, gold diamonds.

"Storm?" Julie gasped, backing away as

she eyed the young wolf's muscular body, huge paws, and big sharp teeth.

"Yes, it is still me, Julie. Do not be afraid. I will not harm you," Storm said in a deep, velvety growl.

And then, before Julie had time to get used to seeing Storm as his majestic real self, there was a final blinding flash of light and Storm appeared once more as a tiny, helpless, gray and white puppy.

Julie blinked hard. "Wow! That's so cool. What a fantastic disguise!"

Storm looked up at her from the floor and she noticed that he was beginning to tremble all over. "My disguise will not fool Shadow. He is looking for me. I need to hide now."

Julie bent down and reached out her hand. Storm sidled up close. He sniffed her hand and then licked her fingers with his warm, pink tongue. Julie's soft heart went out to the scared, little pup. Storm was amazing as his real self, but as a tiny, helpless puppy with fuzzy, gray and white fur and the brightest midnight blue eyes she had ever seen, he was totally irresistible.

"I'm taking you back to my gran. She'll

know what to do. Just wait until I tell her all about you," she decided, picking him up.

"No!" Storm woofed. He twisted around to look up into her face. "No one must know my secret. You must promise never to tell anyone, Julie!"

"Okay," Julie said quickly, to reassure him. She really wished she could have told Gran, who was great at keeping secrets, but if it meant her magical, new friend would be safe, she was prepared to agree. "I'll just say that you're a stray or something."

Storm nodded. "Thank you, Julie."

The shopkeeper came out of the back room with a box in his arms and put it on the counter. "Hello there. Did you

find what you wanted?" he called.

"Oh . . . er . . . yes, thanks. I'll be right there," Julie said, quickly putting Storm down. "Maybe you'd better hide and then you can slip outside with me when I leave," she whispered to Storm.

Storm nodded. "That is a good plan." He quickly scampered under a rack of postcards.

Julie grabbed a loaf of bread and a plastic container of milk from the fridge. As she went to pay for them, her mind was racing.

A few moments ago, she'd been lonely and fed up and wondering how she was going to get through the next few weeks. Now she had the most amazing new puppy friend anyone could wish for!

Chapter
THREE

"Oh my goodness!" said Gran as Julie
came into the sitting room with Storm
in her arms. "Wherever did you get that
puppy?"

"I . . . um . . . found him outside the
shop. He was all by himself. I'm sure he's
a stray, so I told him . . . I . . . um . . .
mean I've decided to take care of him,"
Julie said, quickly correcting herself.

"Now don't go getting carried away,
sweetie," Gran said in a sensible tone. "I
expect his owner's nearby. That puppy

looks like he's been well cared for."

"But Storm was definitely by himself. I had a really good look around. There was no one looking for a puppy," Julie said. "And there's no card in the store window about a lost pup."

Gran nodded thoughtfully. "Well, he's not wearing a collar. Maybe he's a stray after all." She reached out to stroke Storm's fuzzy little head. "Storm, eh? It suits him. Isn't he gorgeous? He looks like an Old English sheepdog puppy to me. But as for keeping him . . . Well, I don't think your mom and dad will be that into the idea."

Julie's heart sank as she realized Gran was right. She'd wanted a pet forever but hadn't been allowed to have one because

no one was at home for most of the day. But Julie had promised to help Storm and she wasn't going to give up that easily.

"It's not fair," she said sadly. "I always have to do what Mom and Dad want. No one ever lets *me* do *anything*!"

She stomped across the room and plonked herself down on the sofa. Storm trotted after her and she picked him up and settled him on her lap.

Storm yawned. "I am very tired. I will sleep now," he yapped. Tucking his little button-black nose under his soft front paws, he closed his eyes.

Julie tensed, amazed that Storm had just spoken, but Gran didn't appear to have noticed anything odd. She stood there, tapping her chin thoughtfully.

Julie leaned over and kissed the top of Storm's fluffy head. "Be careful. Gran almost heard you," she warned him in a whisper.

"Only you can hear me talk, Julie. Everyone else will think I'm barking," Storm woofed sleepily.

Julie sat up again. That was so cool!

Gran checked her watch. "Your mom will be here to pick you up in an hour. I'll have a word with her about Storm. Maybe we can work something out."

"Really?" Julie said excitedly. "Thanks, Gran."

"Now don't get your hopes up. I'm not promising anything," said Gran, reaching for the shopping bag and peering inside. Her eyes twinkled. "Although, those lemon sherbets might have helped."

"Oops." Julie gave a sheepish grin. After finding Storm, it was a total miracle she'd remembered anything from the store!

Julie held her breath and crossed her fingers and toes as her mom sat with a cup of tea on her lap. *Please, please,*

please let her agree to me keeping Storm, she thought.

". . . and I wouldn't mind having Storm here in the daytime, when school starts. I miss dear old Snowdrop. And it would be good exercise for me to take him for dog walks," Gran was saying.

Snowdrop was Gran's beloved miniature poodle, who had died over a year ago.

Mrs. Harding sipped her tea. She wore her beautiful, dark green work suit and a white blouse. "I hadn't banked on having a puppy, but I suppose Storm would be company for Julie during the holidays," she mused. "If you'll have him when we're not at home, Mom, it might work out."

"So we can keep Storm?" Julie burst

out, unable to keep quiet any longer.

Her mom smiled. "On two conditions. Storm goes to the vet for a checkup and if someone claims him as their lost puppy, we hand him over—no arguments."

"Fine!" Julie was prepared to agree to

anything. She gently scooted the sleepy puppy over onto the sofa cushion and then went and threw her arms around her gran and her mom in turn.

"Yay! That's *so* amazing. Thanks, Mom. Thanks, Gran. You're the best!"

"We'd better get going," Mrs. Harding said. "I need to stop at the store to get something for dinner. We can get some dog food and other treats, too, while we're there. Can you carry Storm out to the car?"

"Sure thing! Come on, sleepyhead! We're going home," Julie whispered as she gently scooped Storm into her arms.

Storm stretched, pushing against her T-shirt with stiffened front legs and then he leaned up to lick her chin. "Thank you, Julie," he woofed gratefully.

Mrs. Harding wrinkled her nose. "Don't let him do that, dear. And I don't want Storm in your bedroom until the vet's checked him over. He's probably riddled with worms!"

Storm sat bolt upright. "I do not have worms!" he yapped indignantly.

It was all Julie could do not to burst out laughing at the look on his little gray and white round face.

C h a p t e r
FOUR

The following day, Julie woke up
early, too excited to sleep any longer. She
was about to fling herself out of bed and
run straight down to the garage, where
her mom had insisted Storm sleep.

But something warm and furry was
curled up in the crook of her arm.
"Good morning," woofed a bright little
voice.

"Storm?" Julie exclaimed. "How did
you get up here? Mom will go nuts if she
comes in and finds you on the bed!" She

turned over to cuddle Storm and began
stroking his fluffy, gray and white fur.

Storm gave her a mischievous doggy
grin. "I have used my magic so that only
you can see me."

"Wow! You can make yourself invisible,
too?" Julie said. Storm was just full of
surprises. She wondered what else her
magical little friend could do.

Later on that morning, Julie stood outside her gran's, waving as her mom pulled away from the curb. "See you this evening!" she called.

While her mom was at work, Gran was taking Julie and Storm to get Storm checked out by the vet. After that he could officially sleep in Julie's room.

Gran had arranged a small pet carrier. "It used to be Snowdrop's. It should be just the right size for Storm."

Julie nodded. "Good idea."

As Gran was getting her jacket, Storm eyed the carrier warily. "I do not think I want to go into a cage," he barked.

"People usually take their dogs to the vet in a carrier. You won't have to be in it for long," Julie explained.

"Very well," Storm woofed. He still didn't look too happy, but he allowed Julie to lift him into the carrier and fasten the door.

It was only a short walk to the vet. The waiting room was filled with a variety of people and their pets. While Gran gave their details to the receptionist, Julie sat on a chair with the pet carrier on her knees.

A boy about her own age was sitting opposite her. He had a head of floppy, dark hair. His little black mongrel puppy kept weaving in and out of his owner's legs, getting his leash in a terrible tangle.

Julie grinned. "He looks like a handful," she said to the boy.

The boy shook his head. "Tell me

about it!" He frowned at the little dog.
"Teddy. Sit!" he ordered, but the puppy
ignored him and dived under his chair.

"Julie Harding?" called a nurse from
one of the treatment rooms.

"That was quick." Julie smiled at the
boy and his puppy on her way past. She
placed the carrier with Storm in it on the
examination table. Gran followed her in.

The vet smiled at Julie. She wore a
white coat and had short, black hair,
smooth, dark skin, and twinkly eyes.
"What can we do for you, young lady?"

"Mom says Storm has to have a
checkup. We just got him," Julie said.
"He's a stray, but I'm sure there's
nothing wrong with him."

The vet nodded. "You're probably

right, but it's smart to make sure with a new puppy." She opened the carrier and lifted Storm out. "Hello, Storm. You're an adorable puppy!"

Storm allowed the vet to check his eyes and teeth and part his fur to look

for fleas. He even let her roll him on to his back and pat his round, little tummy.

"Well, he's a fine, healthy pup with no obvious problems," the vet said. "He's about the right age for his first vaccination. As he's a stray, I don't think he's had it. I could do that now, if you like?"

"Um . . . I'm not sure." Julie stiffened. She hadn't expected this.

"What is a vaccination?" Storm woofed.

Julie quickly checked that Gran was speaking to the nurse and the vet was busy tapping Storm's details into a nearby computer. "It's an injection to stop you from getting diseases. Is that okay?" she whispered.

"Injection?" Storm frowned in puzzlement.

Julie didn't expect that any of the magical wolves in the Moon-claw pack had ever visited a vet. Before she could elaborate, the vet reached up to a shelf and turned back to the table. She was holding a syringe with a long needle.

Storm's eyes widened in alarm. He stiffened and laid back his ears. "I do not need this medicine! My magic protects me," he barked.

"Hold him still, please. He's bound to wriggle a bit," the vet said. The nurse grabbed Storm and held him firmly.

"No, wait! Don't give it to him!" Julie cried. "He said that . . . I mean, I don't think . . ."

"It's all right, sweetie. I hated it when Snowdrop had injections, too," Gran

interrupted gently. "The vet won't hurt
Storm. She knows what she's doing."

No, she doesn't, Julie thought
desperately. *Storm's not like any puppy
she has ever treated! He's not even from this
world!*

But there was no way she could explain
without giving away Storm's secret and,
anyway, she doubted if anyone would
believe her.

Suddenly, Julie felt a strange, warm tingling sensation down her spine as miniature, gold sparks twinkled deep within Storm's fuzzy, gray and white fur.

Something very strange was about to happen.

Chapter
FIVE

To Julie's complete amazement the vet and nurse jerked their hands away from Storm as if they'd both been stung. In a stream of golden sparkles that only Julie could see, they shot backward across the room, as if they were on roller skates.

Gran took a step back in surprise as Storm did a giant leap off the examination table and landed on the floor, on all fours, right beside the door.

"Let me out!" he yelped.

As Julie moved toward him, another nurse popped her head into the room. Storm saw his chance. He dodged around her and shot into the waiting room.

The vet and the nurse stood there with stunned expressions. They began blinking and rubbing their eyes as if they were coming out of some kind of trance.

"Storm's just . . . a bit nervous. We'll . . . um . . . make another appointment when he's calmed down," Julie burbled. "Bye! I have to catch him!"

Julie rushed out and sprinted across the waiting room. The receptionist, the boy with the little black mongrel, and the other pet owners gaped at her, but Julie ignored them all.

Storm was pawing frantically at the

front door. "It's all right. I'm here," she crooned, picking him up and taking him outside. "I'm sorry you were so scared. The vet didn't understand that you aren't a normal puppy and I couldn't really explain, could I?"

Storm blinked up at her from under his brow. "You did your best, Julie. Do not worry. I am fine now!"

Julie breathed a sigh of relief. "I'm glad you could use your magic without giving yourself away."

Gran emerged from the waiting room with the empty pet carrier. "Oh, thank goodness. You caught him! I've never seen a dog jump like that before. Maybe we should change Storm's name to Skippy!"

"Who?" Julie asked, puzzled.

"Skippy. He was a kangaroo in an old TV series," Gran explained. "Anyway, I had a quick word with the vet. She says we can bring Storm back any time for his vaccination."

"Um . . . right," Julie murmured. She guessed that there was no way anyone would get Storm to go back there now, but she didn't say so.

"In the meantime, the vet did say Storm was healthy, so that should satisfy your mom," Gran reasoned. "Why don't you take Storm for a walk now to calm him down. There's a park just around the corner. I'll just drop this pet carrier back off at my apartment and meet you there in a few minutes."

"Okay. Thanks, Gran." Julie was relieved—she wasn't sure that Storm would be able to magic himself out of trouble at the vet's a second time!

They walked back with Gran to the old shoe factory building, but then carried on toward the park. As soon as they came to the wrought-iron park gates, Storm gave a happy woof and ran inside.

Julie smiled as she watched the tiny

puppy rooting around in the grass and searching for interesting smells. Storm picked up a twig and came lolloping toward her with it in his mouth. As Julie strolled along, Storm pranced beside her, proudly holding the twig.

Some way ahead, Julie noticed the same dark-haired boy with the small, black dog from the vet. The little dog was on a leash.

"It's the boy from the waiting room and that's his puppy, Teddy," Julie told Storm. "Should we go and say hello?" Julie hadn't had a friend who was a boy back at her old school, but this boy had seemed friendly and it would be nice to know someone her own age in this town.

Storm nodded and dropped his twig, wagging his tail eagerly.

The boy looked up and smiled as they approached. "Hi. Didn't I just see you at the vet's? I'm Isaac."

Julie smiled back. "I'm Julie and this is Storm."

"Hi, Storm," Isaac said, bending down to stroke Storm. "He's a gorgeous puppy. What happened back there? I saw Storm sprint out of the examination room and then you ran after him!"

"Oh, that. It was . . . er . . . just a mix-up. It's sorted out now," Julie said vaguely, hoping to avoid more awkward questions. She quickly changed the subject. "Teddy's really cute, too. Have you had him long?" she asked.

Isaac glanced down at his shaggy little mongrel puppy. Teddy was still engrossed in sniffing something in the grass and seemed in a world of his own.

"Just a few weeks," Isaac said. He made a face. "It's a bit of a sore point."

Julie was about to ask what he meant, but just then, Storm brushed against Teddy, his stumpy tail wagging as he barked a greeting.

Teddy's head whipped around in surprise. He launched himself at Storm and yanked the leash right out of Isaac's hand.

It happened so fast that Julie, Storm, and Isaac were taken completely by surprise.

"Yipe!" Storm yelped as Teddy

boisterously nipped his ear.

"Bad dog! Come here!" Isaac yelled at
Teddy.

Still growling playfully, the little mongrel
bounced down on to his front legs. Teddy
eyed Storm warily, but seemed a bit
calmer now that he'd checked Storm out.

"I said, 'Come here!'" Isaac roared, but
his puppy ignored him.

Julie took matters into her own hands.
She stepped boldly between the two
puppies and clapped her hands loudly.
Storm jumped sideways in surprise, but
Teddy just looked up at Julie to see who
was standing in his way.

"That's enough!" she scolded, frowning
angrily and shaking one finger at the little
mongrel.

Teddy rushed toward his owner with his tail between his legs. Isaac immediately grabbed the leash and pulled Teddy to heel.

"Oh gosh. I'm sorry! I hope Storm isn't hurt," he said, red with embarrassment.

"Of course he is. Your dog just bit him!" Julie snapped, too shaken up and worried about Storm to be polite. "Can't you control Teddy? Come here, Storm. Let me check your ear."

Storm padded over and sat down obediently. "Do not worry. It is not serious," he woofed.

Julie examined his ear. There was a tiny cut where one of Teddy's teeth had caught it. "It's bleeding a little bit," she told Isaac. "I'll have to take Storm back to my gran's apartment and get his ear cleaned up. She lives in the factory apartments."

"I'll walk along with you—it's the least I can do," Isaac said in a subdued voice. "I live at the Gatehouse on Fern Avenue. It's opposite the old shoe factory building."

Julie picked Storm up as they set off, just in case Teddy felt like leaping on him again. But although the little mongrel strained at his leash and kept looking up at Storm, his tongue was lolling out in a friendly grin.

Julie was puzzled. Teddy seemed like a completely different dog now. They all walked through the park gates in silence and emerged on to the street.

Isaac chewed his lip and looked miserable. "I'm really sorry," he apologized again. "I try to get Teddy to behave, but I'm terrible at it. Dad thinks he's just too strong-willed for me. Yesterday, Teddy chewed a corner of our new rug. Mom nearly freaked out. And now this. Please don't tell anyone what just happened."

Isaac looked genuinely upset and Julie felt her anger starting to drain away.

"Well, okay. I wouldn't want to get you into any more trouble," she agreed.

"Aw, thanks," Isaac said, relieved. He dropped to his knees in front of Teddy and took the puppy's little face in both hands. "You're one shaggy little ball of trouble, aren't you?"

Teddy wagged his tail and licked Isaac's chin.

Julie's heart softened. There was no doubt that Isaac loved his little mongrel puppy.

"Why can't you ever behave yourself? You're never going to be let out of your cage," Isaac said sadly to Teddy.

Cage? Julie didn't believe what she had just heard. She was too stunned to react.

But Storm wasn't. His head came up and

a tiny growl rumbled in his throat. "That is not right. Dogs do not live in cages!"

Julie's mind whirled. No wonder Teddy was so badly behaved if he was kept shut up. Any dog would have lots of pent-up energy to get rid of.

"Yoo hoo!" called a familiar voice.

Julie saw Gran coming down the street toward them. She waved to her. "That's my Granny Harding," she said to Isaac.

"Sorry I was held up, sweetie," Gran said as she reached them. "A friend just called me and I had a tough time getting away." She smiled at Isaac. "You're the boy from the vet, aren't you? I'm glad to see that Julie's made a new friend. Maybe you'd all like to come back and have a snack—"

"Gran," Julie interrupted quickly. "Storm hurt his ear. We have to clean it and put some cream on it."

"Oh no. How did that happen?" Gran said, frowning.

"It was an accident. He caught it on something in the grass," Julie lied.

Isaac shot her a grateful look.

Gran bent down to look at Storm's ear. "It must have only been a scratch. It's already drying up," she said as she stood up. She smiled at Julie and Isaac. "Well, should we go, you two?"

Isaac looked uncomfortable. "Thanks very much for the invitation, Mrs. Harding. But I . . . er . . . have to get home. Maybe some other time? I'll see you around, Julie," he said, edging away.

"Bye," Julie said, watching Isaac cross the road and head for Fern Avenue, with Teddy pulling at his leash.

"He seems like a nice boy," Gran commented.

Julie didn't answer. Isaac had seemed really nice. She had started wondering if they might become friends, but now she was confused. There was no way she could ever like a boy who allowed his puppy to be kept in a cage.

Chapter
SIX

Two mornings later, Julie was busy in the kitchen making breakfast as a Saturday treat for her mom and dad.

As the toast popped up out of the toaster, Julie sighed. She hadn't been able to stop thinking about Teddy. Was the little mongrel shut up in a small cage right now?

"What are we going to do about Teddy?" she asked Storm.

Storm was sitting curled up on a chair,

watching as Julie placed the breakfast things on a tray.

His bright midnight blue eyes glinted. "I have a plan! We will go and rescue him."

"Really?" Julie said, doubtfully. "How can we, without anyone noticing? And then what are we going to do with Teddy? Just let me take this up to Mom and Dad and then you can tell me what you have in mind. Okay?"

Storm nodded.

As Julie folded the morning papers under one arm and went into the hall, she didn't see the mischievous look on the tiny puppy's face.

Upstairs, Julie knocked on her parents'

bedroom door before going in. "Here you go! I thought you'd like breakfast in bed," she said.

Her mom sat up looking sleepy-eyed. "Thanks, honey. That's sweet of you."

There was a grunt from beneath the mound of covers and her dad peeked out. His hair was all standing on end. "You're a star, Julie."

"I'm just going to take Storm out for a walk. See you later," Julie told them.

"Don't go too far. And remember to keep him on his leash. You don't want him running into the road," her mom cautioned.

Julie nodded, although she knew that her magical little friend would never do anything so dangerous. Storm was already

waiting by the front door when she
padded downstairs.

Julie slipped Storm's new collar
and leash into her shorts pocket. "I'd
better take these. We're supposed to
be pretending that you're an ordinary
puppy—" She stopped suddenly, as
she felt a now familiar warm prickling
sensation run down her spine.

She saw bright gold sparks igniting in
Storm's fluffy gray and white fur and
the tips of his ears were crackling with
electricity.

"What's going on?" she asked him,
intrigued.

But Storm gave her a mysterious doggy
grin. Lifting one fuzzy little paw, he
sent a glittering burst of power toward
her. A golden mist spun around Julie.
She felt a sense of lightness flicker all
through her body. There was a *whoosh* of
movement and then she and Storm were
flying straight *through* the front door and
zooming upward into the air together.

"Wow! This is amazing!" Julie couldn't
contain her excitement at what was
happening. She held out her arms as they

drifted along above the streets and houses. Storm's gray and white fur rippled in the breeze and Julie's hair streamed out behind her.

"Where are we going, Storm?"

"You will see very soon," replied Storm mysteriously as his little puppy ears flapped in the wind.

They flew above treetops and almost brushed the top of a church spire. Julie spotted the old shoe factory and then they began drifting downward toward a detached old-fashioned, red brick house.

Julie's feet touched grass as she landed beside Storm. They were in a back garden, with neat paths and flower beds.

An idea suddenly popped into Julie's head. "Is this Isaac's house?"

Storm nodded enthusiastically. "We are going to take Teddy to a new home!"

"Hang on a minute . . ." Julie began, not sure that Storm had really thought this through. But with another *whoosh* of gold sparks they were shooting through the house walls.

"Oof!" Julie breathed as they silently exploded into a large, modern kitchen. It had lots of cabinets and stainless steel things. There was a nice table and chairs at one end.

Luckily, the kitchen was empty. Part of the floor was taken up by a roomy wire cage with a cozy bed inside and dishes for food and water. Dog toys were all around. Teddy was curled up on a fleecy blanket, his paws twitching as he slept.

Julie frowned. She had expected to find Teddy shut up in a small cage inside a garden shed, but this cage looked more like a really fancy pet hotel.

Just then, Julie heard footsteps coming toward the kitchen. She and Storm were going to be discovered at any second!

"Quick, Storm. Do something!" Julie whispered.

Just as the kitchen door began to open, there was a tiny flash of gold light and Julie felt herself tingling all over. There was a collapsing sensation and the table and chair legs seemed to shoot up around Julie like giant trees.

Storm had made them the size of mice!

Quick as lightning, Julie and Storm scuttled behind a chair leg. They watched as a giant woman in a robe, who Julie guessed was probably Isaac's mom, forked dog food into a bowl and opened the cage to put it inside. "Here you go, boy," she said.

Teddy's nose twitched as he smelled the food. He leaped out of bed, tail wagging, and started to chomp the food.

Isaac's mom bent down to watch him.

"I hope those new puppy-training classes are going to work. Isaac really wants to keep you and we do, too. If you weren't so destructive in the house, you wouldn't have to sleep in your cage, would you?" She sighed. "I do hope we don't have to find you a new home. It'll break Isaac's heart."

"She seems really nice, doesn't she?" Julie whispered to Storm.

Storm nodded.

Julie felt a stir of guilt. "We got it all wrong, didn't we? Teddy might be a real problem pup, but Isaac and his mom and dad are being really good to him."

"Teddy does not need to be rescued," Storm woofed in agreement, looking as shame-faced as Julie.

Isaac's mom went and opened the back door into the garden, before returning to the kitchen and opening cabinets. Fresh air and sunlight poured into the room.

"Come on," Julie urged, seeing their chance. She sped toward the back door on her tiny legs and scrambled down the step and into the garden. Storm ran alongside her.

Once outside, they hurried along the path that led to the back gate and out of view of the kitchen. There was a faint stretching sensation and a noise like a squeaky balloon and Julie and Storm were normal size again.

"That was so cool!" Julie said, looking forward to flying home magically again. She stretched her arms out in a mock Supergirl pose. "Let's go, Storm!"

But it was too late.

"Hey! What are you two doing here?" called a voice from above them.

Julie looked up to see Isaac peering down at them from his open bedroom window.

Chapter
SEVEN

"I didn't think I'd see you and Storm again so soon!" Isaac said, sounding pleased.

"Er . . . no," Julie said, her mind racing. "We came over to see if you and Teddy . . . um . . . wanted to meet up later or something," she improvised.

Isaac grinned delightedly. "Yeah, great idea. Maybe we could—" His face dropped as he seemed to remember something. "Mom's arranged for me to take Teddy to training classes this afternoon. You wouldn't want to come to that, would you? It might be good for Storm, too," he said hopefully.

"I do not need training!" Storm yapped indignantly.

"Sounds like Storm's saying he'd love to come!" Isaac guessed.

Julie bit back a grin as Storm frowned and laid back his ears. "Maybe we could just come and watch," she said tactfully. "Where's it being held?"

"The community center, next to the church. It starts at 2 PM."

"I know where that is. Okay, I'll check with my mom. If I'm coming, I'll see you there. Gotta go now," Julie said as she remembered that her mom and dad would soon be wondering where she'd gone. She

unbolted the garden gate, which opened
directly into the side road.

"How did you two get in here, by the
way?" Isaac asked, sounding puzzled.

Julie thought quickly. How was she
going to explain the locked gate? "I'm a
good climber! Couldn't resist it," she said,
quickly slipping outside and closing the
gate.

There was no one in sight and they
couldn't be seen from Isaac's house.
Across the road, a thick hedge screened
the other houses. Once again Julie felt the
light feeling spread through her as golden
sparks swirled around and she and Storm
zoomed up into the air.

They were back home in no time. Her
mom was just walking down the stairs in

her nightgown, her hair still wet from the shower.

"Did you have a good walk?" Mrs. Harding asked.

"Yes, thanks," Julie said casually. She told her about bumping into Isaac and the dog-training classes. "I said I might see Isaac there. Is that okay?"

"Of course it is. I'm going shopping later, so I can drop you and Storm off. We can meet up afterward if you like and come home together." Her mom smiled. "I'm glad you're starting to make friends here."

Julie smiled back, happy to know that Isaac looked after Teddy properly. "Me too!"

"Put that puppy on a leash! At once, please!" A voice boomed as Julie walked into the training session with Storm in her arms. The instructor had her hair in a bun and wore a sleeveless, flowered dress and flat, clunky sandals.

Everyone turned around to look at Julie. Blushing, she placed Storm on the floor and clipped on his collar and leash. "Sorry, Storm. Looks like they have strict rules here," she whispered to him.

"I do not mind being captive for a short while," Storm woofed amiably.

Julie spotted Isaac waving at them from across the room. She and Storm hurried over to him.

"Hi! I'm really glad you came!" Isaac rolled his eyes. "The instructor's a bit of a witch, isn't she?"

Julie nodded. "You can say that again!"

There were about forty owners and their dogs in the room. With people talking and dogs barking, the noise was deafening.

Storm's ears swiveled and he looked up at Julie in concern.

"I assume it'll be quieter once the class starts," Julie said, patting him reassuringly. She noticed that Teddy didn't seem fazed by the noise. He was wagging his tail and pulling at his leash as if he wanted to play with the other dogs.

"Get into a large circle, everyone. Come along," the instructor ordered, waggling her hand at anyone who hung back. "That's it, don't be shy."

Julie didn't dare say that she'd only come to watch. This was the scariest woman she'd ever met. She walked forward and joined the circle. "Come on, Storm. Let's join in. It might be fun," she whispered.

Storm looked doubtful, but he trotted after Julie nonetheless.

"I'm Lucy Jackman, but you can all call me Lucy," said the instructor.

The first exercise was teaching the dogs to walk at heel. Two of Lucy's helpers kept an eye on things and offered words of advice if needed.

"Pull gently on the leash, while saying 'Back' firmly, to bring your dog to heel," one of them instructed.

Isaac tried, but Teddy kept dancing around and trying to bite his leash. He

seemed more interested in all the other dogs and kept lunging at them, his tail wagging furiously.

Julie noticed that poor Isaac soon looked very flustered.

"Next, we'll practice the recall," Lucy said loudly. She explained how owners could teach their dogs to learn their names and to come when called.

Storm was enjoying himself and acting like an obedient pet, but Isaac was having a lot of trouble with Teddy. The little mongrel wouldn't respond when his name was called, no matter how hard Isaac tried.

"It's hopeless," Isaac groaned after another twenty minutes. "Teddy's too boisterous. He's just not paying attention."

"Well, it is only his first training session," Julie commented.

"Yeah, I guess you're right," Isaac said, shrugging.

"I'm going to demonstrate the basic sit and stay now," Lucy said. She walked over to Julie and held out her hand. "May I borrow your puppy?"

"Um . . ." Julie couldn't think of a reason to refuse and she didn't think Lucy would have listened, anyway. "Okay, then," she murmured, handing over Storm's leash.

The trainer jerked on the leash so that Storm lifted his head and high-stepped into the center of the room. Lucy suddenly stopped dead. "Sit!" she ordered, pressing a firm hand on to Storm's back. "Be firm. Your puppy needs to know who's in charge," she said briskly.

Storm blinked in surprise, but lowered his fuzzy bottom and sat down. Lucy smiled in a self-satisfied way. She put Storm's leash down and walked backward slowly, saying, "Stay!"

Storm did a doggy shrug. He yawned
and scratched the fur on his tummy with
one back leg and then got up and ambled
over to Julie.

"I have had enough training now," he
yapped.

"Okay. We'll sit this one out—" Julie
began, reaching down to pat Storm, but
before her fingers even brushed his fur,
Lucy swooped forward and grabbed the
little puppy's leash again.

As the trainer tried to drag him back
into the middle of the room Storm gave
a tiny growl of protest. He laid back his
ears and straightened all four legs, so that
his claws skittered across the wooden
floor.

"Come along now. No unruly little

pup's going to get the better of me!" Lucy said, with a determined glint in her eye.

Julie smiled inwardly. *Do you want to bet?* she thought.

Chapter
EIGHT

Storm threw back his head and suddenly stopped dead.

Lucy was jerked to a halt so abruptly that her clunky sandals knocked together with a loud clatter and she almost fell over her own feet. The trainer turned to Storm, her mouth sagging open in surprise as she tried to work out how a tiny puppy had suddenly become as strong as a fully grown Great Dane!

Sighing heavily, she picked Storm up and tucked him firmly under one arm.

"This is unacceptable! Come along now."

But the annoyed little puppy had a rather unmagical solution to being manhandled.

"Ugh!" Lucy cried as a sprinkle dampened her flowery dress. "He peed all over me!" She put Storm down hastily, reached for a tissue, and dabbed at her dress.

Storm scampered back to Julie and sat

beside her, looking pleased with himself.

"Storm, you are *so* bad!" Julie scolded gently, her mouth twitching.

The rest of the class erupted with laughter, including Isaac. Most of the dogs began joining in, barking and yapping, all except Teddy who danced around on the spot.

"Good for you, Storm!" Isaac spluttered. "That Lucy is so bossy!"

Everyone grew calm and the class continued. The final exercise was retrieval. The puppies were supposed to pick something up and return with it to their owners. Teddy simply grabbed the rubber dumbbell and ran around the room with Isaac at his heels.

"I give up," Isaac puffed, red-faced,

coming over to sit beside Julie and
Storm, who were sitting this one out.

The class ended ten minutes later
and the owners and their dogs all filed
outside. Julie stood talking to Isaac before
she went to meet her mom. Storm and
Teddy stood nose to nose, their tails
wagging companionably.

"Well, that was a lot of good. Not!"
Isaac said gloomily. "Teddy was as
naughty and boisterous as he always is."

"He'll be better next time. You'll see,"
Julie said encouragingly. "Look, he seems
to be quite friendly with Storm now."

Isaac nodded, still looking
downhearted. "That's something, I
guess."

Julie felt really sorry for him. Isaac

tried so hard to get Teddy to behave.

"Do you want to go for a walk across the fields tomorrow afternoon?" she said, hoping to cheer him up.

Isaac brightened up a bit. "Yeah, okay. Do you want to meet outside your gran's apartment after lunch? The field's close to there."

"See you there then! Bye for now." Julie waved as she set off toward the stores to meet her mom.

Julie hadn't been asleep for long that night when she woke abruptly to the sound of growling and snapping. She blinked sleepily. She must be imagining it after having spent all day with mischievous dogs.

But as the dogs continued to bark outside, Julie realized that she wasn't dreaming or imagining it. This was real.

Storm was tucked right under her chin, like a furry scarf, and Julie suddenly sensed that he was trembling all over. As she sat up, Storm gave a mournful whine and ducked under the duvet.

"What's wrong?" Julie asked gently, lifting the duvet to look at him. "Are you sick?"

"Shadow knows where I am! He has put a spell on those dogs outside, so that they will attack me," Storm said in a muffled whimper.

Julie leaped out of bed and peered through a crack in the bedroom curtains. She could see a man standing under the street lamp struggling with two long-toothed dogs. Their pale eyes glinted in the moonlight.

As she watched, the man scolded the dogs and got them under control. Their scary faces seemed to soften. He led them away and the growling and snapping gradually faded.

Julie turned back to Storm. "It's okay. They're gone now. You're safe." She got back into bed and Storm crawled up toward her. Julie gathered his warm, little body into her arms.

The tiny puppy was beginning to calm down, but his big, midnight blue eyes were wide and anxious. "Shadow will send more dogs to attack me. Normal dogs will become just like those you saw outside. I may have to leave suddenly, without saying good-bye," he told Julie.

Julie felt a sharp pang. She couldn't bear to think of losing her little friend. "We could find somewhere else to hide you, then maybe Shadow will give up looking and you can stay with me forever!"

Storm looked at her, his little, round face deadly serious. "I cannot do that. One day, I must return to my own world to help my mother and lead the other wolves. Do you understand that, Julie?"

Julie nodded sadly, but she didn't want to think about being so lonely again. She felt determined to enjoy every single second of her time spent with Storm.

"Let's go back to sleep," she said, changing the subject. "We're meeting Isaac and Teddy tomorrow. That's something to look forward to."

Storm yawned and nodded. He cuddled into the crook of Julie's arm as she snuggled them both into a fold of the duvet.

Chapter
NINE

Isaac and Teddy were already waiting outside the old shoe factory building when Julie and Storm arrived the following afternoon.

"Hi, Isaac. Hi, Teddy." Julie bent down to stroke the little dog's shaggy, black fur. Teddy bounced up and down excitedly, whining and pawing at her. "Too much love! Calm down, boy," Julie laughed. Bending down she gently pushed the boisterous pup away.

Teddy sat down and looked at her quizzically.

"You seem to be able to get him to behave, but he takes no notice of me," Isaac grumbled.

"I must have learned something from dog-training class after all. Even if Storm didn't!" Julie said.

She and Isaac laughed as they remembered what a disaster it had been.

"That Lucy woman was a nightmare, wasn't she? I hope it's a different trainer next time," Isaac said as they started walking.

The field was only five minutes away, in the opposite direction of the park. Once there, Julie and Isaac let the puppies off their leashes. Storm and

Teddy immediately rushed around trying to sniff out rabbits.

Julie and Isaac walked along, chatting and enjoying the warm sunshine. Bright yellow dandelions dotted the grass and pillowy clouds floated across the blue sky.

To one side of the field, Julie could see a big sign and a high wire fence around some partly built houses. The fence had been bashed down in one place. As it was a Sunday, there was no sign of any workers or heavy machinery.

Teddy suddenly spotted a rabbit that was heading for the gap in the fence. He flew after it and ran headlong on to the building site.

"Teddy! Come here! It's dangerous over there!" Isaac called, breaking into a run.

Julie wasn't surprised when Teddy just kept on going. Storm ran up to her. "Do not worry. I will go and fetch Teddy," he panted.

Storm tore off ahead of them both as Julie ran to catch up with Isaac.

By the time Julie pounded up to the building site there was no sign of either puppy. Isaac was already standing there, looking around. "Where are they?"

Julie shook her head. "I don't know.

I'll go this way. Why don't you look over there?"

"Okay." Isaac set off toward a big pile of sand.

Julie walked past a huge cement mixer, picking her way carefully over scattered bricks and bits of wood that were lying around. She glimpsed a small, black shape scampering toward a plank that had been placed as a makeshift bridge over a deep ditch.

It was Teddy, and Storm was hot on his trail.

"Over here!" Julie yelled to Isaac, waving her arms.

Isaac appeared as Julie ran toward the ditch. She saw Teddy reach the plank bridge and scamper straight across. Storm bounded after him, but skidded on some mud.

With a yelp of alarm, he plunged into the ditch. There was a splash as the tiny puppy fell into the muddy water at the bottom and sank out of sight.

"Storm!" Julie screamed as Storm's mud-covered little form rose into view again. Coughing, he began splashing around and searching for something to rest his paws on in the sticky earth.

Isaac rushed up, his eyes wide with horror.

Julie realized that Storm probably couldn't use his magic without giving himself away. She didn't think twice. Thrusting the plank aside, she jumped into the ditch.

Mud splashed everywhere as Julie landed waist-high in the ditch. Her foot slid against a submerged brick and she gasped as pain shot up her ankle. Ignoring it, she reached down and grabbed Storm. He scrabbled against her, his muddy fur plastering her T-shirt.

"Thank you for saving me," he woofed, mud dripping from his muzzle.

"No problem," Julie said, using a clean bit of T-shirt to wipe mud from his eyes and nose. "I'm just glad you aren't hurt."

"Are you two okay?" Isaac asked worriedly.

"Kind of," Julie said, wincing at the sharp pain in her ankle. Now that Storm was safe, she was starting to feel sick and shaky.

"You are hurt. I will help you," Storm yapped.

"But Isaac . . ." Julie stopped halfway through protesting as she felt a warm tingling sensation in her hands and golden sparks fizzed in Storm's fur, hidden beneath the thick coating of mud.

The pain in her ankle grew warmer and then icy cold and seemed to drain away completely, just as if she'd emptied out a packet of sugar. "Thanks, Storm. I'm fine now," she whispered.

"Can you climb out by yourself if you give Storm to me?" Isaac said, reaching down.

Julie nodded. She handed Storm up to him.

"All right, little fella? That must have been a nasty shock," he crooned.

Julie scrambled out of the ditch and rose to her feet. Teddy came running toward them, his tongue lolling happily. His black fur was covered with sand and brick dust.

Julie quickly grabbed the little mongrel. "Got you!" Isaac passed her Teddy's leash and Julie clipped it on to his collar. "Oh heck. Look at the state of these two!" she said, looking down at the pair of messy pups.

"Have you seen yourself?" Isaac said. "You look like you've had a bath in melted chocolate. And look at my T-shirt. Mom'll go nuts if I come home like this."

Julie nodded. "Mine will, too. What are we going to—Hang on, I've got an idea! Follow me!"

Chapter
TEN

"Hi, Gran!" Julie said ten minutes later, as the apartment door opened. "Surprise!"

"Oh, my goodness! What on earth happened to you?" Granny Harding's eyes widened in shock as she saw the mess they were in. "Okay. Wait there. I'll get some old newspapers. You'd better take off your shoes and then you can carry those pups straight to the bathroom."

Julie flashed Isaac a grin as they padded

through the apartment with their arms full of muddy puppies. "Gran always knows what to do and she doesn't make a fuss like most grown-ups!"

An hour later, Storm and Teddy had been bathed and Julie and Isaac's clothes were in Gran's washing machine. They sat there wearing borrowed bathrobes, taking turns drying Teddy and Storm with the hairdryer.

Storm didn't like the noisy hairdryer, but Teddy didn't seem to mind it. He closed his eyes, enjoying the way the warm air ruffled his scruffy, black fur.

"There. You're all done." Julie stroked Storm's cotton-wool-soft, gray and white fur. "Mmm. You smell wonderful."

Storm gave her an unimpressed look

from under an extremely fluffy bunch of
fur.

Julie and Isaac erupted with laughter.
"Sorry, Storm. But you should see your
face," she apologized in a whisper.

Gran came in from the kitchen and
put a plate of sandwiches, chips, and a
homemade chocolate cake on the table.
"I thought you might like these."

"Thanks, Gran. You're the best!" Julie
said.

"Yeah. Thank you so much, Mrs. Harding," Isaac said politely. "And thanks for being so cool about this."

Gran smiled. "Don't mention it, dear. It's nice for me to have unexpected visitors."

While Isaac finished drying Teddy, Gran produced a box of dog biscuits. She doled them out to the clean, dry puppies. Teddy and Storm lay on the rug, chomping away happily as Julie and Isaac went to sit at the table.

"Dig in, you two," Gran said, pouring cups of tea. "Oh, I've forgotten the knife and forks. Could you get them for me, Julie? They're on a tray in the kitchen."

Julie went into the kitchen and returned with the tray. Just as she was approaching the table, Teddy jumped up, pawing at her legs. "Oh!" Julie stumbled as she tried to avoid stepping on him. The tray of cutlery flew out of her hands. It fell to the ground with an almighty crash, right beside Teddy.

Gran and Isaac almost jumped out of their skins.

"Yikes!" Storm screeched in shock, leaping to his feet with his fur all standing on end.

But Teddy was still nosing around for biscuit crumbs and didn't seem upset at all.

"That's odd," Julie said.

"What is, sweetie?" asked Gran.

"Well," Julie began. "Teddy didn't react at all to the loud noise right next to him. It's as if he didn't hear it . . ." A suspicion jumped into her mind. "Isaac, can you stroke Teddy to distract him for a minute?"

Isaac looked puzzled, but he tickled Teddy's chest. Teddy wagged his tail and nibbled Isaac's fingers.

Julie went and stood behind them. She clapped her hands loudly. Teddy didn't look around and his ears didn't even flicker.

Julie looked across at Isaac. "I think I know why Teddy seems to be such a problem. He's not misbehaving. He could be deaf," she said gently.

"Deaf?" Isaac echoed. "But he can't be. The vet looked in his ears when he checked him over. He would have noticed if something was wrong, wouldn't he?"

"Not necessarily," said Gran. "If Teddy was born that way, there might be no outward sign—it can be easy to miss in puppies. People assume that they don't learn their names or come when they're called because they're young and boisterous or just disobedient."

"Just like Teddy," Isaac said wonderingly.

"Exactly!" Julie thought back. "It makes sense when you think about it. Teddy probably turned on Storm in the park, because he couldn't hear him coming and thought he was being attacked. Teddy didn't react when I clapped my hands, but when he saw me frowning and wagging my finger at him, he got the message! Do you remember?"

Isaac nodded. "He knew he'd done something wrong then, didn't he? And those other times when he seemed to obey you, you were actually looking at him, so he understood what you wanted him to do," he recalled eagerly.

Julie nodded, feeling even more certain

that she was right about Teddy.

Isaac dropped down beside Teddy
and hugged him. "Poor little boy. It's
not your fault. You can't help it, can
you?"

Teddy licked Isaac's face and looked
perfectly happy.

Julie took the opportunity to whisper
to Storm. "What a shame for Teddy,"
she said sadly. "It must be weird living
in a world of silence. Can you use your
magic to make him better?"

Storm put his head on one side. "But
Teddy is not sick. He was born that
way. He is just different."

Julie realized that Storm was right. She
hadn't thought of it like that. Teddy
wasn't suffering. He was a healthy,

happy little dog and his silent world was
quite normal to him.

"Why don't you take Teddy back to
see the vet? She'll tell you if you're right
about him," Gran suggested.

Julie nodded. "Good idea, Gran." She

turned to Isaac. "At least you'll know that there's a reason for the way Teddy is."

A shadow crossed Isaac's face. "Yeah. But it doesn't help much, does it?"

"What do you mean?" Julie asked.

"Think about it," Isaac said miserably. "What's the use of taking Teddy to training classes? He's not going to be able to learn anything if he can't hear instructions. And if he won't do as he's told and keeps chewing things up, Mom and Dad will definitely make me find a new home for him!"

Julie realized that he had a point. It seemed that Isaac and Teddy were facing a whole new set of problems.

Chapter
ELEVEN

"I wonder how Isaac and Teddy are," Julie said to Storm a couple of evenings later. She'd been hoping that Isaac would call when he'd been to the vet, but so far she hadn't heard from him.

Storm nodded. "I am thinking about them, too." He was curled up in Julie's lap while she was reading.

When the phone rang in the hall, Storm immediately jumped down and ran toward it. Julie got up and followed him.

It was Isaac. "Hi, Julie. You were right about Teddy," he said at once. "He is deaf. The vet thinks it's a problem with the nerves inside Teddy's ears. So he was probably born that way."

"Oh," Julie said. This was one time when she didn't feel good about being proved right. "I'm so sorry," she said.

"I was, too, at first, but the vet's been really good," Isaac said, sounding quite cheerful. "She told me that I'll always have to be extra careful with Teddy near traffic and it's going to be really tough to train him. But guess what, she's got another patient who's got a deaf dog, called Flossie, and the owner, Mrs. Norman, has taught her to respond to hand signals."

"That's fantastic!" Julie enthused.

"I know. The vet called her while I was at the office and Mom's taking me and Teddy over to meet them this weekend. Mrs. Norman only lives in the next town."

"Oh, I'm so happy for you," Julie said warmly.

Storm sat on the carpet, a curious expression on his face. Julie gave him a thumbs-up sign and Storm's tail began thumping against the carpet.

"I'm going to be at Gran's tomorrow. Why don't we meet up? You can tell me more about it," Julie suggested. "And I'd love to help you train Teddy . . . um . . . if you'd like me to, that is," she said, trying to be tactful. She knew that Isaac wasn't too happy that she had managed to get Teddy to behave in the past.

"I thought you'd never ask!" She could tell that he was smiling.

Julie replaced the phone. She beamed at Storm as she told him what Isaac had said.

"I am glad for them both," he woofed.

It was bright and sunny the following morning as Julie and Storm closed the door to Gran's apartment and walked downstairs.

"I'm really looking forward to meeting Isaac and Teddy," she said as they reached the bottom of the stairwell.

But Storm gave a sudden whimper of fear and shot into the side room where the trash cans were stored.

"Storm?" Julie heard loud barking and snarling and glimpsed some large shapes prowling about outside the glass front door. Sunlight glinted off their pale eyes and extra-long, sharp teeth.

Her heart missed a beat. Storm was in terrible danger!

Julie turned and rushed after him. She reached the doorway just as a blinding flash of gold light and a shower of bright sparks lit up the trash room.

Storm stood there, a tiny, helpless puppy no longer, but a powerful, young, silver-gray wolf. His thick neck-ruff seemed to be gleaming with a thousand tiny, yellow diamonds. Standing next to Storm was an adult she-wolf with golden eyes and a gentle expression.

A sob rose into Julie's throat as she realized that Storm was leaving. She'd hoped so much that this day wouldn't come, but she forced herself to be strong for Storm's sake.

"Shadow's dogs are almost here. Save yourself," she urged, her voice breaking.

Storm's midnight blue eyes softened with affection. "Be of good heart, Julie. You have been a loyal friend," he rumbled in a deep, velvety growl.

"I'll never forget you," Julie breathed as a tear rolled down her face.

There was a final burst of dazzling light and big, golden sparks fluttered down around Julie and crackled harmlessly onto the floor.

Storm raised a huge front paw in

farewell and then he and his mother faded
and were gone.

Behind Julie there was a disappointed
snarling. Through the glass door, she saw
three normal-looking dogs padding off
awkwardly in confusion.

Sadness swept through Julie. One golden sparkle lay on the floor. She picked it up and it tickled her palm for a second before blinking out. Julie gave a bittersweet smile. At least she'd had a chance to say good-bye and she would always remember the wonderful adventure she had shared with her magical puppy friend.

"Take care, Storm. I hope you lead the Moon-claw pack one day," she whispered.

Julie squared her shoulders as she went to meet Isaac and Teddy. The two of them were going to need tons of help and support and she was determined to be there for them. A warm feeling spread right through Julie as she realized that there were two new friends in her life to enjoy and she knew that Storm would always be watching over her, wherever he was.

About the Author

Sue Bentley's books for children often include animals or fairies. She lives in Northampton and enjoys reading, going to the movies, and sitting watching the frogs and newts in her garden pond. If she hadn't been a writer, she would probably have been a skydiver or a brain surgeon. The main reason she writes is that she can drink pots and pots of tea while she's typing. She has met and owned many cats and dogs and each one has brought a special kind of magic to her life.